Lawrence Augustus Gobright

Jack and Jill

For old and young

Lawrence Augustus Gobright

Jack and Jill
For old and young

ISBN/EAN: 9783337118945

Printed in Europe, USA, Canada, Australia, Japan

Cover: Foto ©Andreas Hilbeck / pixelio.de

More available books at **www.hansebooks.com**

JACK & JILL

CLAXTON, REMSEN & HAFFELFINGER
PHILADA.

JACK AND JILL.

FOR OLD AND YOUNG.

" 'Tis of books the chief
Of all perfection to be plain and brief."
BUTLER.

BY

L. A. GOBRIGHT,

AUTHOR OF "RECOLLECTIONS OF MEN AND THINGS AT WASHINGTON."

PHILADELPHIA:
CLAXTON, REMSEN & HAFFELFINGER.
1873.

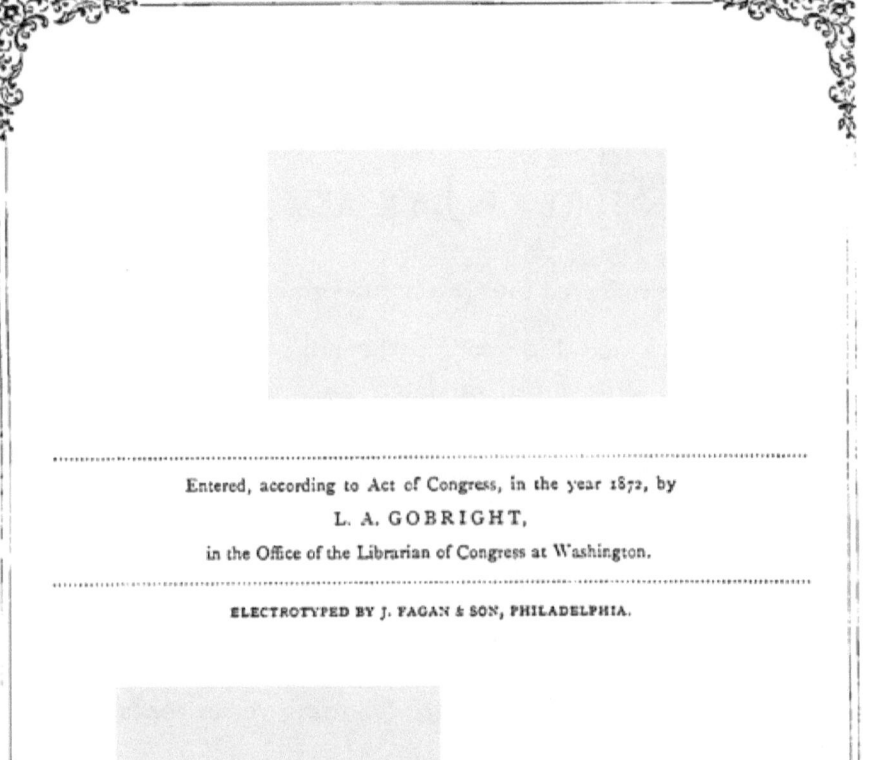

ELECTROTYPED BY J. FAGAN & SON, PHILADELPHIA.

THE

Story of Jack and Jill

Is usually rendered thus in the modern nursery editions :

Jack and Jill went up the hill
To fetch a pail of water,
When Jack fell down, and broke his crown,
And Jill came tumbling after.
Jack up got and home did trot,
As fast as he could caper ;
His brother Bob plastered his knob
With vinegar and brown paper.

And in the earlier editions the following verses appeared :

Little Jane ran up the lane
To hang the clothes a-drying ;
She called for Nell to ring the bell,
For Jack and Jill were dying.
Nimble Dick ran up so quick
He stumbled over a timber ;
He bent his bow to kill a crow,
And shot a cat in the window.

PREFACE.

—◦◦✦◦◦—

"Because the beginning seemeth abrupt, it needs that you know the occasion of these several adventures, for the method of a poet historical is not such as of an historiographer." — Spenser.

THE Nursery Melodies which the author has consulted do not give such information concerning the lives of Jack and Jill as he desired to obtain, in order to write their history with the particularity the subject seemed to demand. Mr. Spofford, the chief of the Library of Congress, extended all the facilities in his power to aid the author, who regrets that he is compelled to assert that the literature in that library, though abundant in other respects, is deficient in the matter of Jack and Jill. Therefore, it became necessary to make inquiries elsewhere — among the private, though not extensive libraries of children. But even there the results were not satisfactory. It was found that the several writers of narratives of Jack and Jill do not agree as to the character of the injury to Jack in the fall. They are, however, in harmony on the averment that his head was repaired by the application of " vinegar and brown paper." Taking this for granted, (and the author has, as yet, discovered no one who doubts the truth,) it is unreasonable to suppose that a broken crown could be repaired with such simple appliances! Therefore, the sensible conclusion is that Jack's head was not broken but merely stunned. As to Jack's " capering " to his home, this would seem to be mere poetic license, not warranted by the facts ; or, it may have been intended to cast ridicule on the event which endangered his life !

By a strange mistake, which cannot be explained, the following inappropriate verse was added to the earlier editions of the history :

> " Nimble Dick ran up so quick,
> He stumbled over a timber ;
> He bent his bow to kill a crow,
> And shot a cat in the window."

Evidently this verse belonged to some other story. The fact is so ap-
parent that the author utterly rejects it, without passing an opinion on its
poetic merit.

The story of Jack and Jill is as truthfully set forth in these pages as the
opportunities for obtaining information warrant ; and the author will ad-
here to this belief until authentic records — not mere logical disquisitions
— shall be produced to convince him of mistake!

The name of Jack is from the French *Jacques*, and Latin *Jacobus ;*
and Jack is the diminutive of John, as understood among ourselves.

Julienne was in vogue among the Norman families. It long prevailed
in England as Julyn, and became so common as Gillian that Jill was the
regular companion of Jack. We have from this the name of Juliana.

Shakspeare, in his play of the "Midsummer Night's Dream," written
about two hundred and seventy-five years ago, alludes to the characters
of Jack and Jill ; and Ray, in his "Proverbs," speaks of them in a pleasant way ; the latter asserting, as a truth, that "a good Jack makes a good
Jill ;" which fact is illustrated in these pages.

Ben Jonson, in his "Gypsies," says :

> "I can, for I will,
> Here at Burley o' the hill,
> Give you all your fill,
> Each Jack with his Jill."

In a note to "Specimens of Lyric Poems," composed in England during
the reign of Edward the First, six hundred years ago, it is said there was
an old play, now lost, called "Jack and Jill."

Researches show that King James I. of Scotland, who died in 1437,
wrote the poem of "Christ's Kirk on the Green," from which it appears
that *Gillie* scorned and made mouths at *Jok ;* which treatment, to say
the least, was unkind, and that Jok "would have loved Gillie" but "she
would not let him." This statement cannot refer to our Jack and Jill,
unless, by an extension of the imagination, it can be supposed that Gillie

PREFACE.

was finally "brought to terms" by Jok, as is sometimes the case in love adventures. It is certain, however, that the royal bard selected these two euphonic names to adorn his poetry, and has linked them with imperishable fame!

The author affectionately requests the readers of this poem to believe that he has undertaken to reconcile probabilities with facts, while discarding the absurdities of compilers, his object being to restore the history to its original seriousness!

> "'Tis not indeed my talent to engage
> In lofty trifles, or to swell my page
> With wind and noise."

For centuries the simple story of Jack and Jill has delighted millions upon millions of children, who, in after years, did not forget the narrative. It has always been pleasant to recall the story, and so it will continue to be in coming time, as long as there is a child in Christendom with the ability to understand the oral relation of the story, or to read it without adult assistance.

The author submits his poem, not to public criticism, but to the judgment of all who appreciate contributions to literature, and especially as his production will, he is sure, fill a vacancy in the libraries of the world, provided the history of Jack and Jill be not rejected in consequence of the ridicule heretofore thoughtlessly cast upon their names!

The narrative should have a place appropriate to the merits of the humble characters never to be separated from English and American memories. The author is certain that the poem will adorn the Library of Congress, as the law requires two specimens of all copyrighted works to be placed within its sacred keeping!

L. A. GOBRIGHT.

WASHINGTON, D. C., 1872

List of Illustrations.

JACK AND JILL.

CHAPTER I.

THE HOME OF JACK AND JILL—THEIR PARENTS—"JOHN ANDERSON MY
JO"—THE HABITS AND OCCUPATION OF JACK AND JILL—THEIR IN-
DUSTRY AND ITS FRUITS—COUNTRY MORALS, ETC.

IN literature we've Jack and Jill,
    Preserved in nursery rhyme,
Of interest now to young and old,
    As in the ancient time.

It is not told where they were born,
    Or who their parents were,
But certain 't is they parents had,
    Who nurtured them with care,

And fitted them as best they could
    To lead a happy life,
That Jack a husband good should be,
    And Jill a model wife.

7

Now, in the walk of humble life,
  And in their married state,
The great and small alike may find
  Much good to imitate.

"John Anderson, my Jo John,"
  A song which you 've heard often,
Which will henceforth, as in the past,
  The soul's best feelings soften,

Tells how John climbed the hill of life,
  By blessings rich attended,
And to the vale, without a fall,
  With his good wife descended.

Alas! not so with reference
  To rustic Jack and Jill,
Who went up slower than they came
  Adown the slippery hill!

From this Burns, maybe, made his song,
  Much everywhere admired,
With such improvements as his Muse
  And kindly heart inspired.

The city has its gayety,
  Where wealth and thrift abound,
And vice and virtue, strongly marked,
  In neighborhood are found.

But many love the country more,
  With its untainted air,
The woodland, and the field, and lawn
  And better morals there.

And in this rural life are hearts
  Which do not vices know;
But virtues which mankind adorn,
  And happiness bestow.

More rich are they with grateful hearts,
  From which contentment springs,
Than those whose e'er increasing wealth
  No true enjoyment brings.

Jack led a strictly moral life,
  Which was a theme of praise,
And everybody wished that he
  Could follow in Jack's ways.

He did not ardent spirits drink
  For artificial cheer,
But was contented with supplies
  Of Jill's refreshing beer.

He ne'er neglected Mrs. Jill,
  Nor close attention paid
To any neighbor's pretty wife,
  Or any comely maid.

No tenpin alley, sample room,
  Or vulgar concert hall,
Could him from his domestic state
  And occupation call.

He owned a little tract of ground,
  To which he gave his toil,
And was rewarded with the fruits
  That issued from the soil.

His cot was plain, but neatly kept
  By Jill, with humble pride,
Who freely whitewash used within
  And on the boards outside.

She planted flower-seeds in the yard,
   Near to the cottage-gate,
And paid attention to the soil
   That they might germinate.

The generous earth its beauties gave,
   Rare, odorous, profuse,
With all the primal colors
   And of variegated hues.

Her cabbages and onions were
   The best her neighbors knew,
With other culinary plants
   Which in her garden grew.

She fed her fowl, she milked her cow,
   And everywhere 'twas said
No woman in the country
   Better bread and butter made.

In all she did, indoors or out,
   She showed good taste and skill,
Which Jack her husband seconded
   With ready act and will.

CHAPTER II.

DOMESTIC COMFORT — RURAL LUXURY — PROOF OF AFFECTION — GOING FOR
THE WATER — THE DRINK — THE CIRCUMSTANCES ATTENDING THE
FALL — MISFORTUNES FROM A COOLING DRAUGHT, ETC.

IN time of summer Jack and Jill,
  Their dinner being o'er,
Sat down to talk and rest themselves
  Before their cottage-door.

The shower that brightened tree and grass
  Had cooled the heated air,
And light winds through the clover-bloom
  Conveyed its fragrance there.

Said Jill "I thirst, I want a drink
  Drawn from our favorite spring,
When Jack replied "I'll water get,
  If you a vessel bring."

Responsive to Jack's readiness
  His loving Jill supplied
The pail, which had been lately scoured,
  And placed it at his side.

As little Mary had a lamb,
  Whose fleece was white, like snow,
And wheresoever Mary went
  The lamb was sure to go;

Jill with devotion quite as strong
  Attended on her Jack,
Who always found her at his side
  Or closely at his back.

Said she "I'll go along with you,
  To cheer you on the way,
Because I care not at this place
  Without my Jack to stay."

Then up they went the hillside steep
  The water to obtain,
But with no purpose at the spring
  To very long remain.

They took a deep and cooling drink,
  And filled the wooden pail,
But on returning to their cot
  Departed from the trail.

Their eyes were turned toward Nature's charms,
  Extending all around,
With dotting flowers upon her robes
  And by the greenwood bound.

Birds resting in their leafy homes
  From weariness of flight,
Upon the beauteous scene looked forth
  And warbled with delight.

The ground being wet with recent rain
  And slippery to the tread,
Jack fell adown the steep hillside
  And struck upon his head!

Jill screamed like any other wife
  Who for her husband feels,
But in her haste to reach her Jack
  She tumbled at his heels.

Alas! this shows that in an hour
  When mortals little think
Misfortune will upon them come
  E'en from a cooling drink!

CHAPTER III.

WHAT JILL DID AFTER THE ACCIDENT — TIMELY ARRIVAL OF ASSISTANCE —
THE ALARM — TOLLING OF THE BELL — WONDERFUL EFFECTS OF VINEGAR
AND BROWN PAPER — THE RECOVERY — THE LESSON.

SOON Jill arose and cried for help,
   Which very soon was found;
The neighbors handled Jack with care
   And raised him from the ground.

They bore him to his cottage home
   And placed him in his bed,
While words gave way to silent grief
   And tears were freely shed.

The news soon flew, both far and near;
   The villagers, alarmed,
Rushed wildly to the scene to learn
   If Jack was sorely harmed!

'Twas then that little Jane, who'd just
   Put out her clothes to dry,
Tore her blonde hair and wrung her hands
   As she began to cry.

23

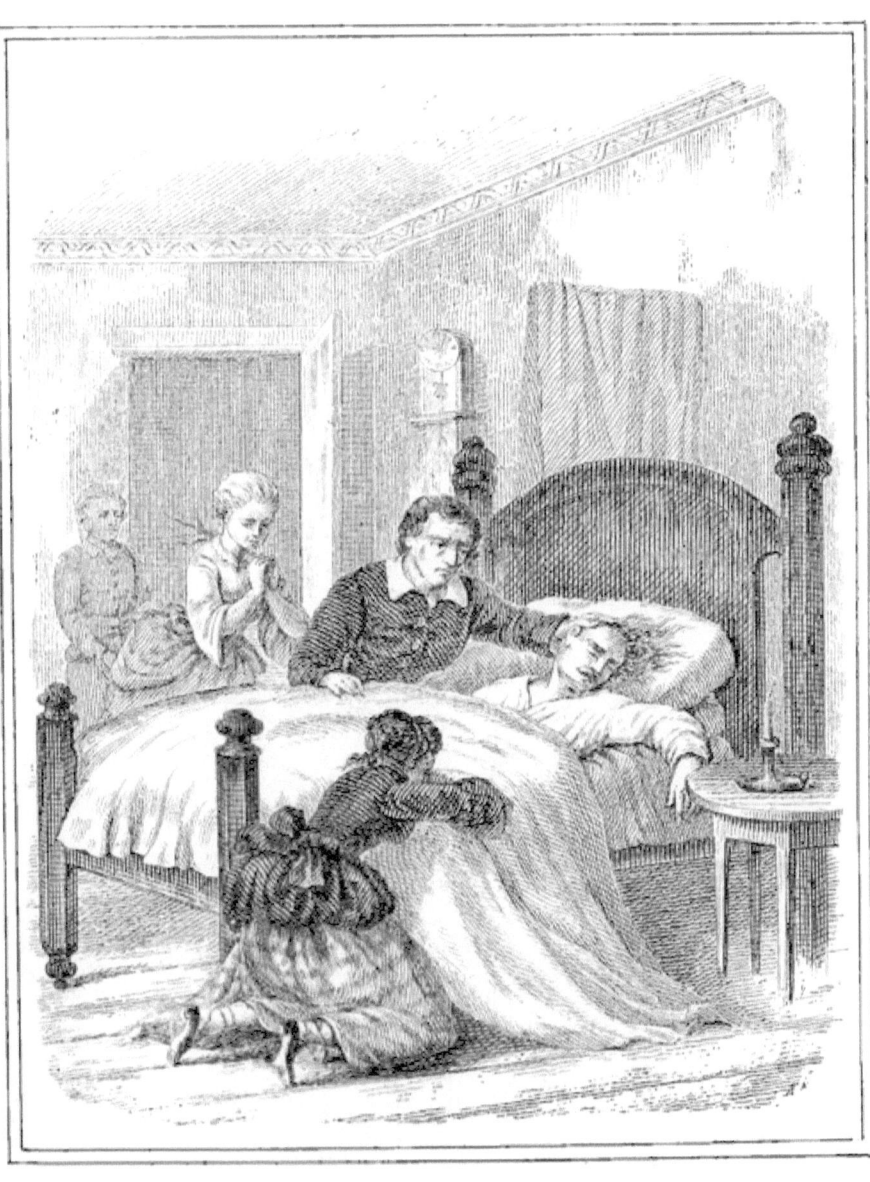

She thought Jack dead, and in her grief
   Implored her sister Nell
To hasten to the village church
   And forthwith toll the bell.

Ah! 'twas a time of deepest woe
   To poor Jack's every friend,
Who thought that he had by the fall
   Come to a fatal end!

Jack had a brother very kind,
   Bob was his common name;
Soon as he heard the tolling bell
   With breathless haste he came.

And bending o'er his brother Jack,
   Feeling his head with care,
He was rejoiced to find no bump
   Nor any fracture there!

Jack gave a sign which showed that he
   Was not among the dead,
And while he groaned in deep distress
   He pointed to his head.

It thus appeared Jack was but stunned —
  E'en this was much deplored —
And that by simple remedies
  He soon might be restored.

Brown paper, steeped in vinegar,
  With confidence was tried,
And was by Bob with tender hand
  To Jack's hurt head applied.

This had a wonderful effect,
  And brought to Jack relief;
There now was no excuse for tears
  Or utterance of grief!

The neighbors all rejoiced that Jack
  Was without any pain,
Or even scratch, and hoped that he
  Would ne'er fall down again!

Jack, now restored to cheerful health,
  Industrious was found,
Attending to his faithful Jill
  And to his farming ground.

He lived for many years in peace
  And happiness with Jill;

Their children meantime played upon
   But ne'er fell down the hill!

Since these events proud governments
   Of glory have been shorn,
And others disappeared in gloom,
   With few the loss to mourn;

While nations weak have grown in strength,
   And e'en our own had birth,
The freest and the happiest
   Existing on the earth.

Though countless names illuminate
   The history of man,
For warlike acts and civic deeds
   E'er since the world began,

No characters are better known
   Than humble Jack and Jill,
With incidents concerning them
   That happened on the hill.

From which a lesson may be learned,
   Of interest to all:
Let them who think that they firm stand
   Take heed lest they shall fall!